ICKY · RICKY 2

THE END OF THE WORLD

← WORM

Written & illustrated by

MICHAEL REX

A STEPPING STONE BOOK™

Random House 🏠 New York

To Sam, for teaching me about funny

Copyright © 2013 by Michael Rex

Photo on page 32 courtesy of John Rader

All rights reserved. Published in the United States by
Random House Children's Books, a division of Random House, Inc., New York.

Random House and the colophon are registered trademarks and
A Stepping Stone Book and the colophon are trademarks of Random House, Inc.

Visit us on the Web!
SteppingStonesBooks.com
randomhouse.com/kids

Educators and librarians, for a variety of teaching tools,
visit us at RHTeachersLibrarians.com

Library of Congress Cataloging-in-Publication Data
Rex, Michael.
The end of the world / written and illustrated by Michael Rex.
p. cm. — (Icky Ricky ; #2)
"A Stepping Stone book."
Summary: "Icky Ricky is up to his eyeballs in trouble and in ick—
giving a funeral for a pizza, dealing with a one-eyed squirrel,
and dressing up as Bigfoot." —Provided by publisher.
ISBN 978-0-307-93169-6 (pbk.) — ISBN 978-0-375-97102-0 (lib. bdg.) —
ISBN 978-0-307-97539-3 (ebook)
[1. Behavior—Fiction. 2. Humorous stories.] I. Title.
PZ7.R32875En 2013
[E]—dc23   2012033884

Printed in the United States of America

10 9 8 7 6 5 4 3 2

Random House Children's Books supports
the First Amendment and celebrates the right to read.

CONTENTS

"Ricky!" Ricky's mom shouted as she pulled into the driveway of their house. "Why in the world are you having a mud fight in my old dress?"

"Because the one-eyed squirrel stole the Palooka Pops!" said Ricky.

"Oh, Ricky . . . please tell the story from the beginning." She didn't bother to get out of the car.

It all started when Gus and Stew and I were at home playing our game called Coach Jackson. Our baseball coach, Mr. Jackson, says one thing over and over. He says, "See the ball! Hit the ball!" That's how he teaches you to hit home runs. Anyway, we were in my room. I had a toy baseball bat, and Stew would throw stuff at me and Gus would be Coach.

WHAM!

SLUG-O

Gus would say, "See the sock! Hit the sock!" And Stew would pitch the sock, and I'd hit it.

Gus would say, "See the toothbrush! Hit the toothbrush!" And Stew would throw the toothbrush, and I'd hit it.

Then he started throwing stuffed animals.

"See the penguin! Hit the penguin!" And I was like, *wham!*

"See the moose! Hit the moose!" And I was like, *wham!*

Then Stew chucked a juice box!

Gus shouted, "See the juice box! Hit the juice box!" And I nailed it across the room! A real frozen rope! It exploded all over my wall.

The doorbell rang. I ran down to answer it, and it was a pizza delivery guy. He handed me a pizza. I told him I didn't have any money, but he said it had been paid for already. He was talking on his phone, and he ran back to his car. Gus and Stew were like, "All right! Pizza!" But I told them that I didn't order a pizza.

We opened it, and it looked awesome. Pepperoni and meatballs! Extra cheese, too! I thought that maybe Dad ordered it, so I shouted, "Dad! Did you order a pizza?"

He was in the garage working, and he said, "No!"

I noticed a piece of paper taped to the pizza box. It read "220 Longview Road." I live at 220 Fairview Road. Gus figured that the delivery guy had brought the pizza to the wrong address.

Then Gus asked, "What if the person who ordered it comes looking for it, and he's like a big biker or something?"

And Stew said, "Yeah! And he just got out of prison and he hasn't had pizza in thirty years!"

I was like, "Yeah! Maybe he went to prison because he's a pizza nut and stole tons of pizzas!"

8

I said I knew where 220 Longview
Road was, and that we should deliver this
pizza to the person who had bought it.

Gus was like, "Yeah. Cool." And Stew
said that maybe the biker dude would be so
happy that he would share it with us and
let us ride his motorcycle. We grabbed the
pizza and ran out of the house.

It was a bit dark and cloudy, but it wasn't raining. We started running down the street, but Gus said he didn't like passing the house with the freaky man-dog. It's a dog that lost some fur around his eyes, so it's kind of skin-colored there, and he looks like a man wearing a dog mask.

THE MAN-DOG!

We turned around and went the other
way. But Stew said he didn't like going
that way because of the one-eyed squirrel.
There really is a one-eyed squirrel that
lives in a tree or something, and it's the
meanest squirrel ever. Once I saw it snatch
a cookie right out of a kid's hand!

THE ONE-EYED SQUIRREL!

We ended up taking a small path that
leads between the houses. We followed the
little stream back there, and finally came
out on the next block. We had about six
blocks to go when we saw some lightning,
and then, *boom!* There was this huge
thunder explosion! It started raining like

crazy. I held the pizza box over my head so
I could stay dry. We ran to find someplace
to get out of the rain.

Gus screamed, "One-eyed squirrel!"
And he pointed to something in the trees.

Then I shouted that we were going the wrong way, so we turned around. But that didn't seem right, so we went another way.

I was getting all confused, when Stew slipped on some mud. I tripped on Stew and fell on the pizza, and Gus landed on top of me.

The box got all bent up. The thunder kept going. *Boom! Boom! Boom!*

We got up and ran toward Silvey Park. I held the pizza box under my arm. We ran until we got to a picnic table and crowded under it.

We opened the box and looked at the pizza.

"Uh-oh," I said. It was a mess. The box had been bent in half and squished, so all of the cheese was stuck to the cardboard. And the box was so wet that the cardboard started to get little soggy holes in it.

"Guys, we destroyed the pizza," Gus said. "It's the worst pizza ever. We can't deliver this."

Stew said, "What should we do?"

I said when it stopped raining, we should go back to my house, fix the pizza and the box, and then try delivering it again. Pretty soon the rain stopped, so we got out from under the picnic table. The bottom fell out of the soggy box and the pizza fell on the ground.

We picked up as much of the box as we
could because we don't believe in littering.
And we scooped up the pizza and stuffed
it in our pockets and carried it home.
Some grass and mud had gotten mixed
up in it. We kept dropping things, like the
pepperonis and the meatballs.

When we got back to my house, there wasn't much pizza left. We emptied our pockets and put it all on the kitchen counter. Stuff that was already in our pockets had gotten all mixed up with the pizza parts. Mine had an eraser stuck in them. Stew had a dollar stuck in his, and Gus found out he had a hole in his pocket and almost all the pizza parts had fallen out.

"Wow," I said. "This pizza really needs some work. But we can do it!"

"Yeah!" said Gus. "You're the best pizza doctor in the world, and it's time to operate!"

I put on my mom's rubber dish-washing gloves and hung a paper napkin over my mouth like a doctor's mask. My face was still wet so it stuck easily. Stew and Gus put napkins on their faces, too.

The first thing we did was push and shove the pizza back into a circle. But it was lumpy and not flat like a pizza should be. I picked out some pieces of grass. Then I got out a rolling pin and rolled it over the pizza. But it all stuck to the roller. We scraped that off and still had a big, messy pile of cheese and crust.

"Excuse me, Doctor," said Gus. "Maybe if the pizza was hot, it wouldn't be so lumpy."

"Good idea, Assistant Pizza Doctor," I said.

We dropped the junked-up pizza on a plate and stuck it in the microwave. I put it on high for five minutes. But after about a minute, it started to pop and make all sorts of noise, so I took it out.

It was really hot and steamy. I rolled it again, and again it just stuck to the rolling pin.

"Maybe we should add stuff to make it more pizza-ish," suggested Stew.

"Yeah," I said.

Now, I had made dough in school when I was in kindergarten, so I knew we needed flour. We poured that on. We needed more

cheese, too, so we looked in the fridge but only found a can of Cheese-in-a-Can. We sprayed that onto the pizza. We couldn't find any tomato sauce, so we squeezed a bottle of ketchup onto the pizza.

We microwaved the pizza again. Then we rolled it again. It still stuck to the rolling pin.

I took the blob in my hands and smushed it all together into one big ball.

"There!" I said. "It's a new invention! People around the world will no longer eat pizza *pies*. They will eat pizza *balls*!"

Gus and Stew looked at the pizza carefully, then looked at me.

"No they won't," they said at the same time.

I looked at the pizza, too. Without saying anything, we all stuck our fingers in it and tasted it. It was awful.

"Doctors," I said, "I think our operation has failed. I think we've lost it."

"Lost what?" asked Stew.

"The pizza," I said. "It's dead. We killed it."

TO BE CONTINUED . . .

ICKY RICKY'S TIP
FOR NEVER BEING BORED! #1

COLLECTIONS

I'm never bored. Never. It's because I have a lot of different interests. One of my favorite things to do is collect stuff. Lots of kids collect game cards or action figures or toy cars, but those can be expensive.

I like collecting stuff I can get for free, like my toenail clippings.

I've been keeping my toenail clippings for as long as I can remember. I also have toenails from my friends, some from my grandma, some dog toenail clippings, and I even have one that I found when my family was staying in a hotel!

You might be saying, "But I *have* a collection. Now what do I do with it?"

Organize it! I organize mine in many different categories.

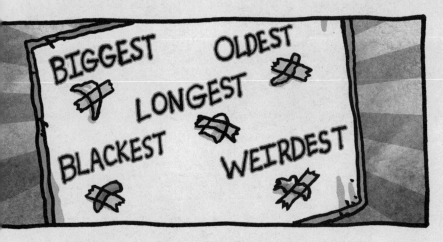

I also like to figure out different ways to display my collection. Right now I have all the clippings taped to a piece of fancy paper. In fact, it looks so great I'm going to hang it in the living room!

CHAPTER 2

THE EGYPTIAN
PIZZA FUNERAL!
(PART 2)
Featuring
PALOOKA POPS,
PIZZA GUTS,
AND THE RETURN
OF THE ONE-EYED
SQUIRREL!

"But I don't understand why you're wearing my old dress, Ricky," said Ricky's mom, still sitting in the car.

So we were all looking at the dead pizza, and then we hung our heads for a moment until I had my best idea of the day.

"Hey!" I said. "Let's give it a funeral!"

"Yeah!" said Gus. "A pizza funeral!"

Then Stew asked, "Where are we going to bury it?"

"In the backyard!" I said as I ran out the back door. Gus and Stew came with me. We looked around and decided on a good spot near the fence. I found a shovel and dug a small hole. The dirt was soft from the rain.

"Hey," said Gus, "maybe we should do it like the Egyptians and bury the pizza with stuff it needs in the afterlife."

I was like, "Wow! That's an awesome idea." We had been studying Egypt in school. When their kings died, they put all this crazy stuff in their tombs for their next life. Like chairs and boats and gold. They even had the dead guy's guts put in jars so he could keep them!

"Hmmm," Gus said. "What does a pizza need?"

"Um . . . a plate! And a knife?" said Stew.

We ran back into the kitchen for a plate and a knife. What else did it need? I looked around the house. "What about a pencil and paper?" I said. "So it can draw if it's bored?" We grabbed a pencil and a sheet of paper.

"What about a ball for playing games?"
said Gus. We grabbed a tennis ball.

"What about a hat if it gets cold?" said
Stew. We found one of my old baseball
hats and took that.

THINGS YOU NEED IN THE AFTERLIFE!

We tried to lift the pizza blob off the
counter, but it kept falling apart. I grabbed
an old doughnut box from the recycling bin
and pushed the blob off the counter right
into it.

"Gus, look!" I said. "A sarcopha-GUS!"
We all started cracking up, and then we
scooped up the stuff that fell on the floor
and put it in an empty can that we found in
the recycling.

"That's his guts," I said. "He needs them
in the afterlife." I carried the box out to the
hole and dropped it in. We put the pizza
guts can in, then the plate, the knife, the
hat, the ball, and the paper and pencil.

"Wait!" said Gus. "It needs a dessert!"

"Pizza doesn't eat dessert," I said.

"Well, it might need a snack in the
afterlife," he said.

We ran back inside to the kitchen.
In one of the lower cabinets, I found my
bag of leftover Halloween candy. It was
all the crummy candy that no one really
eats, like Coconut Waltz bars and Walnut
Crunchability bars and those little stupid
lollipops called Palooka Pops that are
kinda white and all taste the same.

We took the candy and tossed it in the hole, too, and then we piled dirt on top.

"We need a tombstone," said Gus.

We got what was left of the pizza box and stood it up behind the mound of dirt. I found a marker and wrote "R.I.P." on the box.

"What does that mean?" asked Stew.

"Rest in Peace," said Gus.

The tombstone looked pretty good.

Then Stew was like, "So, what do we do at a funeral?"

"We wear black and say nice things about the pizza while crying," I said.

We ran back in the house and went to the basement. I opened up a trunk of old clothes. I gave Stew my dad's black jacket

and pants. I found this old black dress, and Gus got my old black shorts and a black sweatshirt that said "Whazzup?" on it.

We went back outside. It was starting to rain again. It was perfect for a funeral.

"Dearly beloved," I started. I had heard people say that in movies. "Today we are here to bury our best friend, Pizza. He was a good, kind pizza. He had lots of friends and he had lots of pepperoni. He will be missed." I started to fake-sniffle.

Then Stew sniffled and said, "He always helped me when I had a problem. He helped with my homework once. I will miss Pizza."

"I will miss Pizza, too," said Gus. "He helped me fix my bike and took me out to get ice cream." He started to fake-cry and blew his nose on his arm.

"He bought me a race car," I said, starting to fake-cry really hard.

"He bought me a rocket, and we went to the moon," said Gus, fake-crying.

"He bought me a time machine, and we went to the end of the world," said Stew. He blew his nose on his arm, too.

I started weeping really hard and said,
"He bought me a sock."

"Just one?" asked Gus.

"Yeah," I said. "He was a cheap pizza."
I blew my nose on my arm, too.

We all started cracking up.

BOOM!

The thunder crashed again, and a flash of lightning startled us. Then something amazing happened! The one-eyed squirrel dropped out of a tree and started digging away at the pizza grave. We all jumped up and screamed and ran around!

Then I noticed the squirrel didn't want the pizza. It took the crummy Palooka Pops and ran off.

I bumped into Stew, and we fell over, and then Gus fell over, and we got all covered in mud. And then I shouted,

MUD FIGHT!

We started beaning each other with mud. I was like, "See the Gus! Hit the Gus!" And he was like, "See the Stew! Hit the Stew!" And Stew was like, "See the Ricky! Hit the Ricky!"

"See, Mom?" said Ricky. "It makes total sense."

"Well, I guess so," said Ricky's mom. "You did the right thing trying to deliver the pizza."

"But I feel kinda bad about the guy who didn't get his pizza," said Ricky.

"Yeah," said Gus. "Even if he was a pizza thief."

"Don't worry," said Ricky's mom. "When the pizza guy delivers to the wrong house, he has to bring another pizza to the right house. It was his mistake. Now, let's get you cleaned up and ready for dinner."

"Great!" said Ricky. "What are we having?"

BOOGIE TISSUES!

Staying home sick from school can either be really boring or really fun. You just have to be creative with what's around you, even if you are stuck in bed.

Make art! If you have a pile of sticky boogie tissues, squish them together to make a sculpture. Remember, it doesn't have to look real to be good art.

You can also use a bunch of boogie tissues to make a Santa Claus beard. Ho! Ho! Ho!

Organize and display your boogie tissues. Biggest! Wettest! Stickiest! Greenest! (See? Anything can be a collection.)

If you're lucky, your friend is home sick, too, and you can video chat. You can even share your works of art, beards, or collections with each other. However, if you are going to sneeze, aim your nose away from the screen.

"Who are you?" asked the woman with the flashlight. "And why do you look like a pile of mud?" She was standing in a very dark backyard.

"My name's Ricky," said Ricky. "Are you Travis's mom?"

"Yes, I'm Mrs. Murphy," she said. "But

I asked you a question. Why do you look like a disgusting pile of mud, and why are you running through my yard?"

"Oh!" said Ricky. "Because I drank some doughnut-flavored apple juice!"

"Excuse me?" said Mrs. Murphy. She wasn't smiling. "You'd better explain!"

"Okay! Okay!" said Ricky, catching his breath. . . .

Well, it all started today in school. Our teacher, Ms. Jay, had asked if we did anything interesting over the weekend, and Travis said he saw Bigfoot! Everyone was laughing, but Travis kept saying that he saw him. Even I was kind of laughing at first. But the thing is, I don't know Travis that well, and maybe he did see Bigfoot, so I stopped laughing.

And kids were like, "Did you see an alien, too? What about a ghost? What about a leprechaun? What about a UFO?" Travis put his head down on his desk. He looked pretty upset.

Then Ms. Jay asked me if I did anything interesting over the weekend. I started to say that I didn't do anything interesting, but then all of a sudden, I sneezed! Right in front of everybody. It was the hugest sneeze ever. Snot went flying all over my desk. I had all these boogies on my face and everything.

Everyone started cracking up! Except
Travis. He just handed me a tissue while
everyone else was laughing. That's when I
realized that Travis was pretty cool.

Things got calm in class, and we were
getting some work done, and then I had
my best idea of the day. I wrote a note
that said, "Hey, Travis! If you want to see
Bigfoot again, come to the path near Black
Pond at seven o'clock tonight! Bring your
camera!"

I didn't put my name on it, because I
didn't want him to know it was from me.
I didn't even tell Gus and Stew about my
idea. If I really wanted my plan to work,
it had to be a secret.

Later in the day, I put the note on his
desk while he was using the computer.

When Travis read the note, he stood
up and said, "You guys will all be sorry
tomorrow when I bring in a picture of
Bigfoot! You won't be laughing then." But
everyone started laughing again.

When I got home from school, I started
working on the Bigfoot costume. I put on
brown pants, a brown shirt, and my dad's
big brown snow boots. I stuck a big pillow
under the shirt to make me look fat. I didn't
know if Bigfoot was fat, but it looked good.
I dug around in my closet for something
to wear on my head, and I found a big,
crazy wig from when I was a rock star for
Halloween. It was perfect for Bigfoot.

In the closet, I also found a box that
I had forgotten about. It was my pickle
experiment.

Did you know that a pickle is just a
cucumber that has been sitting in this stuff
called brine? I wanted to make my own
pickles, but I didn't have brine so I used
apple juice. And I didn't have a cucumber
so I pickled other things.

I made a pickled doughnut, a pickled brownie, a pickled slice of pizza, a pickled cupcake, a pickled piece of peanut-butter-and-jelly sandwich, and some pickled mac and cheese.

I opened the jar with the pickled doughnut in it. I tried to taste it, but it had turned all mushy in the apple juice. Actually, everything else had gotten soft and mushy. But then I realized I had a new invention! Flavored apple juice!

I tasted the doughnut-flavored apple juice, and it was pretty gross. So were the slice-of-pizza-flavored apple juice and the mac-and-cheese-flavored apple juice. But I tasted them all just in case one of them was awesome.

None of them were. In fact, I couldn't get the taste out of my mouth, so I found some of my dad's minty gum. Usually I don't like that gum, but it helped get rid of the gross taste. I kept sticking more pieces of gum into my mouth until I could barely chew.

I looked at my clock and saw that it was almost seven! I had totally forgotten about my Bigfoot plan. As I ran out of the house, my mom asked me where I was going, and I was like, "Blown blob Black Plond!" because my mouth was full of gum. I tore down to the path by Black Pond.

I never really finished my Bigfoot costume, so I started rubbing mud on my clothes and face and I stuck grass and leaves all over me. A worm was crawling on my head, but it didn't bother me. It was getting dark now, so I figured my costume would look pretty good. I hid behind a tree and waited . . . and waited . . . and waited . . . but Travis never showed up.

TO BE CONTINUED . . .

"Ricky!" called Police Officer Mackey from the road above the sewer ditch. "What the heck are you doing down there, and why are you wrapped in garbage bags?"

"Oh," said Ricky, "because no one in this town litters!"

"What the heck are you talking about, son?" asked Officer Mackey.

"You see," said Ricky, "this is what happened. . . ."

It all started when I went over to Stew's house and brought my Cleanup Day stuff. I knocked on Stew's door and he was ready for Cleanup Day, too. We both had a bunch of big green garbage bags and backpacks filled with water bottles and snacks. We went to get Gus. When we got to his house, he was like, "What's Cleanup Day?"

I told him that everybody in town picks up garbage and stuff, and at three o'clock in the afternoon, you bring everything down to Dumpsters parked at the fire station. Then the town throws an ice cream party for everyone who cleaned up. It's awesome.

Gus said he wanted to help, too. He got some garbage bags and some snacks, and he even grabbed a pair of work gloves in case we had to pick up anything that was really messed up.

We walked down my street looking for garbage. There wasn't any. We went down another street. Nothing.

A lid from a coffee cup blew down the sidewalk. We chased it like crazy, but it was blowing all over. It blew back and forth across the street, and we just couldn't catch it. Finally, we got close to it. We all jumped for it!

I got it.

We sat on the ground. We were sweaty and out of breath. I pulled out a water bottle and took a drink.

Stew opened a can of soda.

It sprayed all over like a geyser and soaked us with soda. I guess the running had shaken it up.

We licked what we could from our arms and around our mouths.

Gus said, "Yummm! Refreshing!" like a guy in a soda commercial.

We started cracking up, but I was like, "We gotta get done by three o'clock if we want to go to the ice cream party."

So we walked down some more streets, finding practically nothing.

Gus picked up a cigarette butt, Stew found a napkin from a doughnut store, and I found a receipt from a gas station. But that was it. Our town is really clean.

"This is boring," said Gus.

"Yeah," said Stew. "I want to pick up lots of garbage."

Then I had a good idea. I opened my backpack and took out the cereal bar that I had packed as a snack. I pulled the wrapper off and threw it on the ground. Gus and Stew were kind of freaked out, because I hate litter.

Then I was like, "Hey, a cereal bar wrapper!" and I picked it up and put it in my bag.

Gus and Stew got what I was doing. They both opened up their snacks and chucked the wrappers on the ground, too. Then they picked them up.

"Hey, I found a cupcake package!" said Stew.

"I got a Mini-Tart wrapper!" said Gus.

Then I had my best idea of the day.
"Why don't we go down to the woods
behind Black Pond?"

"Yeah!" said Gus. "There's tons of
garbage there!"

So we ran off to the woods.

When we got there, we picked up
all sorts of trash. We found a broken
plate, some soggy books, some messed-up
bedsheets, a bunch of rope, and a rusted-
out bucket. We each filled a big bag with
trash.

We were really getting into it, and we
walked deeper into the woods than we
normally did. The farther we went into the
woods, the more our feet sank in the mud,
but we kept going. That's when we saw the
greatest thing ever!

I was like, "Whoa!"

Gus said, "Oh yeah!"

And Stew said, "All right!"

It was a junky, rusted-out, beat-up car!
The whole thing! And it had no tires!

I said, "We have to clean this up!" We
started pushing and pulling on the car, but
we figured out that it wasn't going to move.

"I don't think we can bring it to the fire station," I said. "It's too heavy."

"Yeah . . . we would have to be like superheroes to move it," said Gus.

I jumped into the front seat and said, "Maybe we can drive it there!" And I started fake-driving and screaming and stuff.

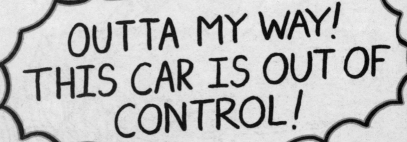

Then Gus jumped on the hood of the car. "Mister! Slow down! I need a ride to the doctor! I swallowed an umbrella!"

And then I said, "Get in! I'll get you to the hospital!"

Then we both screamed like I was driving really fast.

Then Stew jumped in front of the car.
He put his hand up like a policeman.

"Stop right there!" he shouted. "You're
going two hundred miles over the speed
limit!"

"But, Officer, he swallowed an
umbrella, and I have to get him to the
hospital!" I screamed.

"Well, why didn't you say so?" shouted
Stew, and he got in the car, too.

I fake-drove like crazy, and Stew
hung out of the window, shouting, "Out
of the way! Out of the way! Official
police business! This man swallowed
an umbrella!"

"Oh no!" I screamed. "We're lost!"

Gus screamed, "Check the GPS!"

I screamed, "This old hunk of crud car is too old for a GPS!" And I jammed on the gas pedal.

"We need a map!" screamed Stew. "We need a map!"

"Look in the glove compartment!" I screamed.

Stew opened the glove compartment,
and a bunch of mice popped out!

We started yelling like maniacs! The
mice were running all over the car! One
mouse ran down the dashboard and across
my back. One jumped onto Stew's head
and then into the backseat. We were trying
to get out and we were bumping into each
other and falling and stuff.

We climbed out of the car and ran.
We jumped up and down and made sure we
didn't have any mice on us or in our pants
or anything. Then we started cracking up.
We're not even afraid of mice, but they
jumped out of that glove compartment like
it was a horror movie.

And then I saw something totally cool. "Hey, guys!" I said. "Look over there!"

The tires from the car were piled up in some bushes. All four!

"We can bring those downtown!" I said.

"Yeah!" said Stew. "We should get going. We don't want to miss the ice cream party at three o'clock!"

We grabbed the tires and rolled them along.

I had two tires and Gus had two tires, and Stew was trying to carry the filled-up garbage bags. He fell over after a minute.

"They're too heavy," he said. "I can only carry one."

"We'll have to leave two here. We'll come back for them later," I said.

"Yeah, but what if someone takes them?" Gus asked.

Then I said, "Who's gonna steal a bag of garbage?"

"A garbage thief," said Stew.

"Yeah," said Gus, "a garbage thief."

Then I was like, "Okay, let's put them in the trunk of the car. No one will find them there." We opened the trunk, and there was only one thing in it. Cool ski goggles!

Gus got them. We put our trash bags in the trunk and closed it, and then we started walking back to town. I rolled two tires, Gus rolled two, and Stew carried his bag of garbage. Our hands were getting black from the rubber, and water was sloshing out of the inside of the tires.

We came to the top of a hill, and all of a sudden the tires started rolling really fast. We couldn't catch them. They were totally out of control, and then they went off this little bump and disappeared.

We went to see where the tires landed.
They were in some greenish water in a
ditch next to a big sewer pipe. It wasn't
deep at all, just kind of thick. Like soup.

"Oh, man!" I said. "We gotta get them
out of there, or we're just rotten litterers!"

I waded into the water, and Stew was
like, "Stop! It's polluted. I heard there are
fish with toes in that water!"

"If you go in there, you'll get mutated,
too!" said Gus.

I had to get those tires out, but I also had
to stay dry somehow. I don't mind getting
wet, but I don't want to turn into a mutant.
I needed something to put over my clothes.

"I know!" I shouted. "We'll make a
hazmat suit!"

"What's hazmat?" asked Gus.

"Hazardous material," I said. "Like stuff
that if you touch it, it will melt your skin or
make you mutate into a mutant!"

I dumped out my backpack and wrapped
the extra garbage bags around my arms
and legs.

Stew started pulling stuff out of his garbage bag. We used the rope to tie the bags on me. Gus gave me his work gloves and the ski goggles. We ripped a hole in one garbage bag and put that over my head, like a shirt. Then I put the broken bucket on as a helmet.

I looked awesome! We didn't have much time to bring the garbage to the fire station if we wanted to go to the ice cream party, so I got right to work.

I went into the water and started to
pull the tires out, but they were heavy and
the insides were all filled with water. When
I handed them to Gus and Stew, the water
sloshed everywhere! It was soaking through
my hazmat suit, and my feet were sinking
into the mud at the bottom of the ditch.

Finally, all four tires were out of the
water, but I felt something strange under
my foot. I reached into the water and
pulled out . . .

A plunger! And as I pulled it up, tons of
water splashed onto Gus and Stew.

Stew started movie-screaming, "Oh
no! I'm a mutant now!" He grabbed a
messed-up sheet from his garbage bag and
wrapped it around his body. Then he put
both of his arms through one sleeve of his
shirt and limped around.

Then Gus pulled his shirt over his head
and stuck his hands out the bottom.

I started screaming, "Alert! Alert! It's
the end of the world! The mutants are
coming! The mutants are coming!"

Gus and Stew ran at me!

And I was screaming, "See the mutant! Hit the mutant!" I swung the plunger at them. We started having an end-of-the-world mutants-versus-the-hazmat-guy battle! It was Mutant World War One! It was epic!

Finally, they got the plunger, so
I dropped a tire over their heads and
trapped them.

"You see?" Ricky said. "That's how we got here."

"Well," said Officer Mackey, "I'm glad you wanted to clean up the town. But I have bad news. Cleanup Day was last week."

"Ohhh . . . ," said Ricky. "That must be why we couldn't find any trash."

"Must be," said Officer Mackey.

"So," said Ricky, "we don't have to get all of this stuff to the fire station by three o'clock for the ice cream party?"

"Nope, sorry," said Officer Mackey. "That was last week, too."

"Great!" said Ricky. "That gives us more time to play Mutant World War Two!"

REPURPOSING

"Repurposing" means finding something that is old and using it for something new. I've been doing this my whole life but didn't know it had a name!

If you have a sock and can't find the one that matches it, it can be repurposed as many things. It can be a soft lunch box that you hang from your belt, or it can be a sleeping bag for a fish.

SLEEP TIGHT!

If you have an old stuffed animal that is losing its stuffing, cut grass makes a great replacement.

Old baby food jars can be used to store little, important things, such as a collection. Their tight lids and high-quality glass make for a museum-quality display. Here's my collection of old Band-Aids!

CHAPTER 5

THE MOST
AWESOMELY
PERFECT BIGFOOT
PLAN
(PART 2)
Featuring
THE EGG-THROWING
LADY AND THE RETURN
OF THE MAN-DOG!
Guest-Starring
THE GUM-EATING
DUCK!

OR GOOSE!

Ricky stood dripping in Travis's backyard.
Travis's mom held the flashlight's beam
right on his face.

"I'm sorry," said Mrs. Murphy, "but
I still don't understand why you're in my
yard, and why you are soaking wet."

Travis never showed up. I got worried that if he didn't get the picture, everyone would laugh at him even more. So I decided to go to his house. I knew what street he lived on but wasn't sure which house was his.

I started walking down the street, but I didn't want anyone to see me because Bigfoot doesn't just walk down the street. So I snuck into someone's backyard and went through all the backyards toward where I thought Travis lived. That was a big mistake. The first yard I went into, I was face to face with the man-dog!

It barked like crazy! I ran from the dog and jumped over a fence into the next yard. *Wham!* I plowed right into a grill and the charcoal spilled all over me, which was actually pretty cool for my costume. The dog jumped up on the fence behind me, and I ran to the next fence and climbed over that.

I stopped for a moment to catch my breath. Then I heard a lady screaming. She was like, "Get out of my yard, you freak!" I guess I did look pretty freaky, especially in the dark.

And then she started throwing eggs at me. She had good aim and totally beaned me! But I was wearing the pillow, and it didn't hurt.

I ran again. The next yards were divided by bushes, so I just kind of shoved my way through. I tripped and my gum fell out of my mouth. Then the weirdest thing ever happened!

A duck, or a goose, took my gum. It was dark so I couldn't tell what it was, but it seems that the people who lived in this house had a duck, or a goose, instead of a dog or a cat or something. The duck, or the goose, started running around with my gum.

But that got me worried, because it would make sense that a duck, or a goose, doesn't know that you shouldn't swallow gum. With that skinny little neck, that big piece of gum could choke the duck, or the goose, so I had to get it back.

I chased the duck, or the goose, all over. When I got ahold of the gum, it just stretched out, and the duck, or the goose, went one way and I went the other.

Finally, the gum snapped, and I fell back into a pond! Not only did these people have a duck, or a goose, they had a pond in their backyard with these big goldfish in it! The fish were flopping all over, and I could swear a fish went in my pants!

Luckily, no one came out of the house. I got out of the pond. The duck, or the goose, dropped the gum, which was even weirder (because it was delicious!), and I grabbed it.

The duck, or the goose, must have thought we were playing because it started chasing me. I put the gum back in my mouth because I needed both hands to climb the next fence. I ended up in this yard, and then I fell over that playhouse and bounced over that trampoline, and that's when you found me.

"You did all of this for Travis?" asked Mrs. Murphy.

"Yeah," said Ricky. "He helped me out, so I figured I should help him out."

"That's very nice of you. But Travis is at karate class right now. That's why he couldn't go to Black Pond."

"Oh," said Ricky.

"But he should be home soon," said Travis's mom.

Just then, they heard a car pull into the driveway in the front of the house.

"That's Travis. He's home!" said Mrs. Murphy. "You stay right here! This will be fun!"

She started screaming like she was in a horror movie. "Help! It's Bigfoot! In our yard! Heeellllp!!" While she was screaming, she pulled her phone from her pocket and held it up to take a picture.

"Help! It's Bigfoot! Help!" she screamed. She looked at Ricky and whispered, "Make some Bigfoot noises!" Ricky started to growl and moan.

Travis and his dad came running from
the front of the house.

"Don't worry, Mom! I'll save you!"
shouted Travis. His dad stopped running,
but Travis didn't.

Travis went right for Ricky and gave him a giant, flying karate kick in the stomach! Travis's mom snapped a picture!

Ricky went flying back into the bushes, and then he got up and ran away. Behind him he could hear Travis's mom still using her movie voice, saying, "My hero!"

Ricky was glad he had worn the pillow under his shirt.

THE NEXT DAY . . .

The next day when Ricky got to school,
a bunch of kids were standing around
looking at something. Ricky pushed into
the group. Travis was showing everybody
a picture of him in the air, karate-kicking
something that looked like a monster.

"It doesn't look like Bigfoot, but it sure
is freaky," said one kid.

"Yeah! I guess you really did see
something," said another kid.

"Dude! You totally kicked its butt!" said a different kid.

"That looks like a pretty awesome battle," said Ricky.

"Yeah, it was," said Travis, smiling in class for the first time since before he mentioned Bigfoot.

"Awesome," said Ricky.

"Yeah, awesome," said Travis.

Ricky walked away from the crowd of kids. He covered his mouth because he didn't want anyone to see his huge smile. A worm fell out of his hair, and that gave him a great idea for a new collection.

119

WORMS I HAVE FOUND IN MY HAIR!
July 4th
Hallo ween
Stew's sleepover
Mom's Birthday!
July 4th (#2)

ICKY RICKY 1

TOILET PAPER MUMMY

If you love mud, earwax, sludge, boogers, and other gross things . . . then you'll love

Illustrations © 2013 by Michael Rex